Caesar
the No Drama Llama

Written and Illustrated
by Bee Dugan

Caesar the Llama
Was tired of all the drama.

He made up his mind,
said goodbye to his mamma,

And decided to go find
a place with no drama.

He first went up
to see the birds,

But was sad
to hear
some unkind
words.

He then went down
to visit the fishes,

But was disappointed to hear words that were vicious.

He looked high and low
and all around,

But a place with no drama
could not be found!

After days of searching,
tired as could be,

Caesar gave up and sat down
under a tree.

At first he was happy
without all the noises
Of shouting and growling
unhappy voices,

But then in the silence
he realized he missed
Laughing and singing,
the sounds of happiness!

Just when he was feeling
particularly blue,
He heard a voice say,
“Can I sit with you?”

He turned to see, to his surprise

A friendly man with twinkling eyes!

Caesar followed the man into town
And watched him spread kindness
all around!

It was then that everything
became crystal clear:
Your heart can't be open
if it's closed with fear.

Love is not something
that's here or there.
Love is something
you bring to share.

The End

Caesar
the
No
Drama
Llama

and his friends
Bee Dugan

and Larry McCool.

About the Author: Author and illustrator *Bee Dugan* has a degree in music education and has worked with children of a variety of ages. She has been lucky enough to spend time with Caesar the No Drama Llama, which helped her create this book.
She lives and works a stone's throw from the beach, at Cannon Beach, Oregon. She is an avid follower of Christ. This is her first book.

About the Llama: *Caesar the No Drama Llama* is a therapy llama who travels with Larry McCool around the Pacific Northwest. His mission is to spread good vibes and give amazing hugs! You can follow his real-life adventures on Instagram and Facebook.

One Printers Way
Altona, MB R0G 0B0
Canada

www.friesenpress.com

First Edition — 2021

ISBN
978-1-03-912013-6 (Hardcover)
978-1-03-912012-9 (Paperback)
978-1-03-912014-3 (eBook)

1. JUVENILE FICTION, STORIES IN VERSE

Distributed to the trade by The Ingram Book Company

CPSIA information can be obtained
at www.ICGtesting.com
Printed in the USA
LVHW071652230722
724093LV00018B/46